WONDER BOOKS®

Charles Schulz

A Level Two Reader

By Cynthia Klingel and Robert B. Noyed

The Child's World®

Charles Schulz drew great cartoons. He created the "Peanuts" comic strip.

Charles Schulz in front of his "Peanuts" drawings

Charles was born in Minnesota on November 26, 1922. He grew up in the cities of Minneapolis and St. Paul.

Minneapolis at the time Charles grew up there →

Charles was a smart boy in school. He liked to read cartoons and comics. Most of all, he loved to draw.

After high school, Charles spent time in the army and worked at many different jobs. He also married his wife, Jean.

Charles with his wife, Jean →

Charles began drawing cartoons of children. A Minnesota newspaper ran his first comic strip, called "Li'l Folks."

Charles sold the comic strip to other newspapers. People liked "Li'l Folks." The name of the comic strip was then changed to "Peanuts."

Charles Schulz after getting an award for his "Peanuts" cartoons

14

On October 2, 1950, the first "Peanuts" comic strip was printed in nine newspapers. Charles kept drawing "Peanuts" until he died on February 12, 2000.

Charles Schulz smiling

Everyone has come to love the "Peanuts" gang. They love Charlie Brown, Snoopy, Lucy, Sally, Linus, Schroeder, Peppermint Patty, and all the others.

Charles Schulz with Charlie Brown, Lucy, and Snoopy →

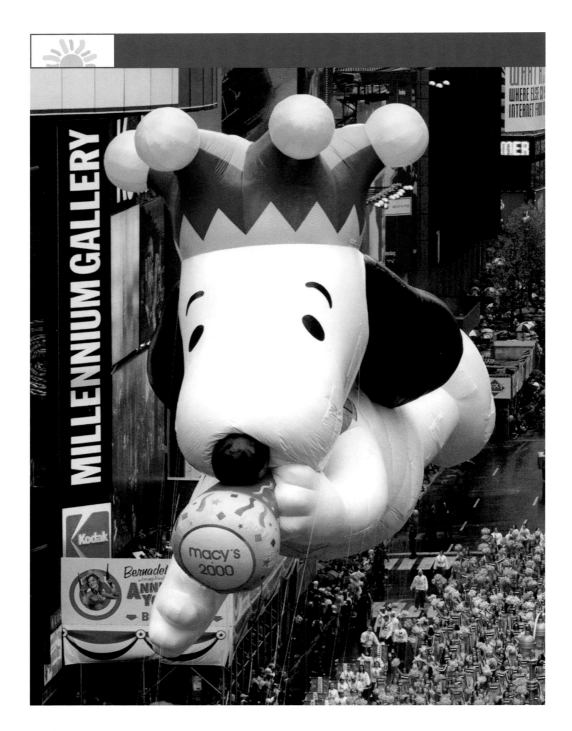

18

"Peanuts" has been made into television shows, plays, and movies. Snoopy even has his own balloon in a Thanksgiving Day parade.

A Snoopy balloon at a Thanksgiving Day parade

Charles Schulz brought enjoyment to many people. His cartoons will always make people smile.

Snoopy with young fans →

21

Index

To Find Out More

Books

Mascola, Marilyn. *Charles Schulz: Great Cartoonist.* Vero Beach, Fla.: Rourke Publishing, 1989.

Schulz, Charles Monroe. *Funny Pictures: Cartooning with Charles M. Schulz.* New York: HarperCollins Children's Books, 1996.

Web Sites

The International Museum of Cartoon Art
http://www.cartoon.org/
For information about the Boca Raton, Florida, museum that has many works by Charles M. Schulz.

The Official Peanuts Web Site
http://www.snoopy.com
For information about Charles M. Schulz and the "Peanuts" gang.

22

Note to Parents and Educators

Welcome to The Wonders of Reading™! These books provide text at three different levels for beginning readers to practice and strengthen their reading skills. In addition, the use of nonfiction text gives readers the valuable opportunity to *read to learn*, not just to learn to read.

These leveled readers allow children to choose books at their level of reading confidence and performance. Level One books offer beginning readers simple language, word choice, and sentence structure as well as a word list. Level Two books feature slightly more difficult vocabulary, longer sentences, and longer total text. In the back of each Level Two book are an index and a list of books and Web sites for finding out more information. Level Three books continue to extend word choice and length of text. In the back of each Level Three book are a glossary, an index, and a list of books and Web sites for further research.

State and national standards in reading and language arts emphasize using nonfiction at all levels of reading development. The Wonders of Reading™ books fill the historical void in nonfiction for primary grade readers with the additional benefit of a leveled text.

About the Authors

Cynthia Klingel has worked as a high school English teacher and an elementary teacher. She is currently the curriculum director for a Minnesota school district. Writing children's books is another way for her to continue her passion for sharing the written word with children. Cynthia is a frequent visitor to the children's section of bookstores and enjoys spending time with her many friends, family, and two daughters.

Robert Noyed started his career as a newspaper reporter. Since then, he has worked in communications and public relations for more than fourteen years for a Minnesota school district. He enjoys writing books for children and finds that it brings a different feeling of challenge and accomplishment from other writing projects. He is an avid reader who also enjoys music, theater, traveling, and spending time with his wife, son, and daughter.

Published by The Child's World®, Inc.

PO Box 326
Chanhassen, MN 55317-0326
800-599-READ
www.childsworld.com

Photo Credits
© AFP/Corbis: 10, 13, 14, 21
© AP/Wide World Photos: cover
© Bettman/CORBIS: 2, 5, 6
© Chuck Jackson/CORBIS: 9
© Reuters NewMedia, Inc./CORBIS: 17, 18

Project Coordination: Editorial Directions, Inc.
Photo Research: Alice K. Flanagan

Library of Congress Cataloging-in-Publication Data
Klingel, Cynthia Fitterer.
Charles Schulz / by Cynthia Klingel and Robert B. Noyed.
    p. cm.
Includes index.
ISBN 1-56766-950-6 (library bound : alk. paper)
1. Schulz, Charles M.—Juvenile literature.
2. Cartoonists—United States—Biography—Juvenile literature.
[1. Schulz, Charles M. 2. Cartoonists.]   I. Noyed, Robert B. II. Title.
PN6727.S3 Z76 2002
741.5'092—dc21

                    2001000449